Sally and the Elephant

Written by Ruby Corbet • Illustrated by Isabel Lowe

D1285731

Sally met an elephant.

2

She took it home to tea.

3

She took it to the drive-in.

She took it to the sea.

She took it on the jungle gym.

She took it on the slide.

Then Sally and the elephant

ran away to hide!

8